seriously SILLY Colour

Laurence Anholt · Arthur Robins

The Little Marzipan Man

ORCHARD BOOKS

There was once a silly old lady
and a silly old man.

The Little
Marzipan Man

For Joe Cleere,
with Seriously Silly wishes
L.A.

For Rosie, with love
A.R.

Visit Laurence Anholt's website at
www.anholt.co.uk

ORCHARD BOOKS
338 Euston Road
London NW1 3BH
Orchard Books Australia
Level 17/207 Kent Street, Sydney, NSW 2000

First published in Great Britain in 2009

Text © Laurence Anholt 2009
Illustrations © Arthur Robins 2009

The rights of Laurence Anholt to be identified as the author
and of Arthur Robins to be identified as the illustrator
of this work have been asserted by them in accordance
with the Copyright, Designs and Patents Act, 1988.

A CIP catalogue record for this book is available from the British Library.

ISBN 978 1 84616 079 0 (hardback)
ISBN 978 1 84616 318 0 (paperback)

1 2 3 4 5 6 7 8 9 10 (hardback)
4 5 6 7 8 9 10 (paperback)

Printed in China

Orchard Books is a division of Hachette Children's Books,
an Hachette UK company.
www.hachette.co.uk

"I am hungry," said the silly
old lady.
She went to the cupboard to
look for some food, but the only
things she could find were . . .
two peas, a sausage, some
watercress, and a lump of
old marzipan.

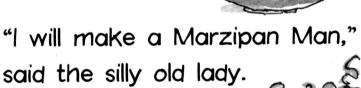

"I will make a Marzipan Man,"
said the silly old lady.

But the silly old lady didn't listen.
She put the Marzipan Man
in the oven.
When he was ready, the
Marzipan Man hopped out
onto the silly old man's plate.

Eat me, eat me,
As quick as you can.
I'll be yummy in your tummy,
I'm the Marzipan Man!

"Ee-urgh!" grumbled
the silly old man.

Without taking a bite, the silly old man ran out of the kitchen and into the lane with the little Marzipan Man running behind.

At the bottom of the lane, the Marzipan Man saw a playground. It was full of monkeys with purple bottoms.

"Perhaps they will eat me,"
thought the Marzipan Man.

Eat me, eat me,
As quick as you can.
I'm better than bananas,
I'm the Marzipan Man!

The monkeys picked up the
Marzipan Man and passed him
from paw to paw.
"BLEURGH!" they shouted.

Nobody will eat the
Marzipan Man.

The monkeys ran after the silly
old man with the Marzipan Man
chasing behind.

The Marzipan Man hadn't gone
far when he saw a giant looking
very hungry indeed.
"I'm sure he will eat me,"
thought the Marzipan Man.

Eat me, eat me,
As quick as you can.
I'm yummy as honey,
I'm the Marzipan Man!

The giant picked up the Marzipan
Man on the tip of one finger
and held him close to his
enormous nose.

POOH!
Nobody will eat
the Marzipan
Man!

The giant dropped the Marzipan
Man onto the grass and they
all ran into the forest with the
Marzipan Man running behind.

The forest was dark and cold.
"How I wish someone would eat
me," cried the poor Marzipan
Man, rubbing his little green eyes.

It began to snow. In the middle of the woods, the Marzipan Man saw Father Christmas.

"Perhaps he would like to eat me," thought the Marzipan Man.

Eat me, eat me,
As quick as you can.
I'm a sweet little treat,
I'm the Marzipan Man!

Father Christmas cracked his whip and set off as fast as his reindeer could carry him. The giant, the monkeys and the silly old man sat beside him in the sleigh.

"Come back! Come back!" called
the Marzipan Man.
At the end of the path was
a huge lake.

But the sleigh flew up in the air
and high over the lake.

"How will I ever cross that lake?"
said the Marzipan Man. A tear
dripped off his sausage nose.

Just then, a funny head popped
out of the water.
It was a Marzipan-Eating Monster.

So the Marzipan Man hopped
onto the tip of the monster's tail
and they swam across the lake.

The water was dark. The water
was deep. The Marzipan Man felt
damp on his toes . . .

The water reached
his marzipan ankles.

The water
reached his
marzipan knees.

The water reached
his marzipan bottom.

The water
reached his
sausage nose.

And the Marzipan Man hopped
onto the monster's head . . .

Eat me, eat me,
As quick as you can.
I'm as yummy as your mummy,
I'm the Marzipan Man!

And he hopped into the monster's
enormous mouth.

"WHOO-EEURGGH!" bellowed the
monster.

WATERCRESS!
I HATE WATERCRESS!

And he spat him out so hard
that the Marzipan Man shot
high into the air . . .

. . . across the lake . . .

over the forest . . .

. . . past the playground . . .

up the lane . . .

. . . in through the window . . .

. . . and straight onto the
silly old lady's plate.

"Marzipan!" said the silly old lady.
"My favourite!"

She put in her false teeth and swallowed the Marzipan Man up in one big bite.

ENJOY ALL THESE
SERIOUSLY SILLY STORIES!

Bleeping Beauty	ISBN 978 1 84616 311 1
The Elves and the Storymaker	ISBN 978 1 84616 312 8
The Silly Willy Billy Goats	ISBN 978 1 84616 313 5
The Ugly Duck Thing	ISBN 978 1 84616 314 2
Freddy Frogface	ISBN 978 1 84616 315 9
Handsome and Gruesome	ISBN 978 1 84616 316 6
The Little Marzipan Man	ISBN 978 1 84616 318 0
The Princess and the Tree	ISBN 978 1 84616 319 7

All priced at £4.99

Orchard Books are available from all good bookshops,
or can be ordered from our website: www.orchardbooks.co.uk,
or telephone 01235 827 702, or fax 01235 827 703.